RABBITS ON ROLLER SKATES!

by Jan Wahl

with pictures by David Allender

RABBITS ON ROLLER SKATES!

by Jan Wahl

with pictures by David Allender

• Crown Publishers, Inc. • New York •

*Text copyright © 1986 by Jan Wahl. Illustrations copyright ©
1986 by David Allender. All rights reserved. Published by Crown
Publishers, Inc., 225 Park Avenue South, New York, New York
10003 and represented in Canada by the Canadian MANDA Group.
Manufactured in Hong Kong. CROWN is a trademark of Crown
Publishers, Inc.*

*Library of Congress Cataloging in Publication Data
Wahl, Jan.   Rabbits on Rollerskates   Summary: Rhymed text
and illustrations follow the progress of a group of rabbits
on roller skates. [1. Rabbits—Fiction. 2. Roller-skating—Fiction.
3. Stories in rhyme] I. Allender, David, ill. II. Title
PZ8.3 W133Rab 1986   [E]   85-9679   ISBN 0-517-56997-3
10 9 8 7 6 5 4 3 2*

A special howdy-do to Nicholas and Manton Hurd.
For Brooke.—D.A.

Here they come!
Here they come!

Rabbits on roller skates!
Rabbits on roller skates!

Jumping, bumping,

Leaping, creeping.

Rabbits on roller skates!

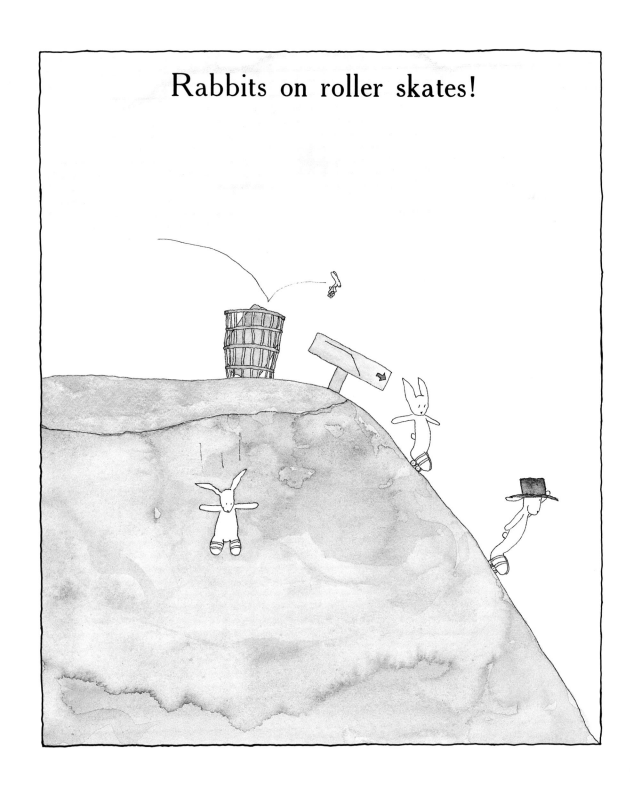

Rabbits on roller skates!

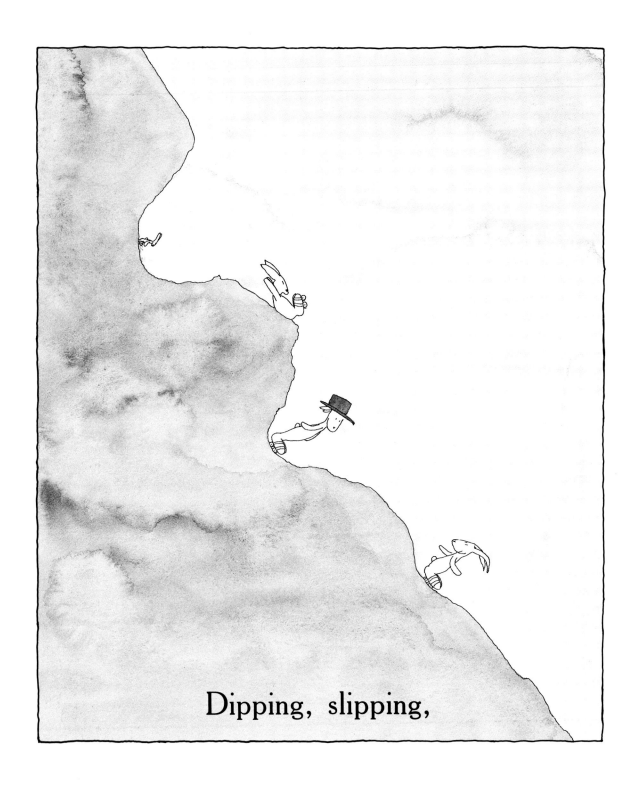

Dipping, slipping,

Dashing, splashing.

Rabbits on roller skates!

Rabbits on roller skates!

Falling, crawling,

Flopping, plopping.

Rabbits on roller skates!

Rabbits on roller skates!

Over the fence,
Wash on the line.

In the haystack —
Eight or nine.

Rabbits on roller skates,
Now without a spill.

Rabbits on roller skates,
Climb a high hill.

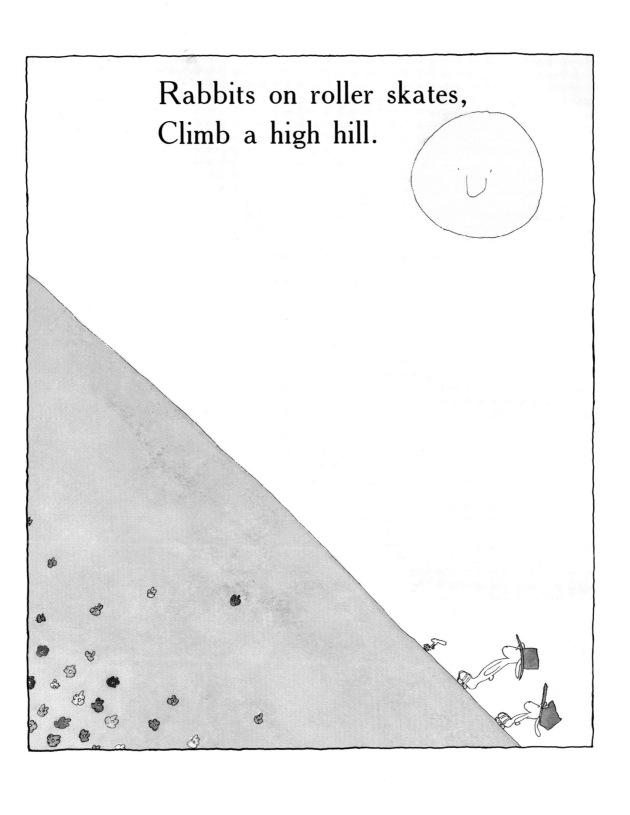

Huffing, puffing,
WHOOSH, they go!

Always fast, never slow.

Rabbits on roller skates,
Through the night.

Rabbits on roller skates –
What a sight!

THE WINNERS!

Rabbits on roller skates,
Across the lawn.

Rabbits on roller skates,
Gone! Gone! Gone!